Tessa Snaps Snakes

Alison Lester

For Jill

Houghton Mifflin Company
Boston   1991

Laughter

Ernie laughs when his mouse runs down his shirt.

Celeste laughs at the clown.

Rosie laughs with her baby sister.

Nicky and Tessa giggle under the hose.

Frank laughs at his
favorite TV show.

But Clive laughs when he surprises his mother.

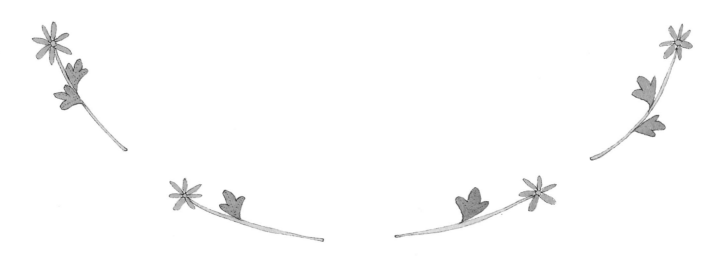

Pocket Money

Nicky does odd
jobs.

Ernie has a pet
shop.

Frank has a paper
route.

Crocodile Cakes

Celeste works in
the garden.

Clive has a cake
stand.

Tessa collects cans.

But Rosie runs a circus.

Nicky has a secret hiding place.

Ernie sleeps with his tortoise under his pillow.

Tessa has an invisible friend.

Frank locks his
diary.

Rosie visits her
pony at night.

Clive has a hidden
treasure.

But Celeste investigates her mother's wardrobe.

Dislikes

Celeste dislikes
muddy dogs.

Nicky hates taking
medicine.

Ernie doesn't like
his boots leaking.

Rosie can't stand
wearing dresses.

Clive doesn't care
for piano practice.

Tessa hates her
itchy orange
sweater.

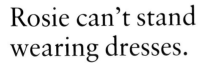

But Frank loathes his new haircut.

Messages

Clive uses a
walkie-talkie.

Tessa mails a letter.

Frank uses signal
flags.

Celeste has a
private telephone.

Rosie makes smoke
signals.

Ernie has a carrier
pigeon.

But Nicky writes in the sky.

 # Fears

Frank is afraid of mice.

Celeste is afraid of thunder and lightning.

Clive is afraid of big dogs.

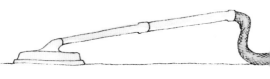

Rosie gets
frightened crossing
the bridge.

Ernie is afraid of
the dark.

Nicky is scared of
spiders.

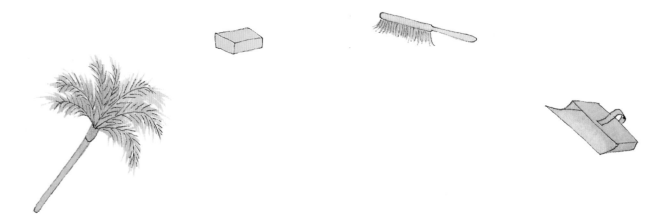

But Tessa is afraid of the vacuum cleaner.

Fancy Dress

Tessa is a tiger.   Clive is a crocodile.   Frank is a rocket.

Nicky is a witch.

Rosie is an
envelope.

Celeste is an angel.

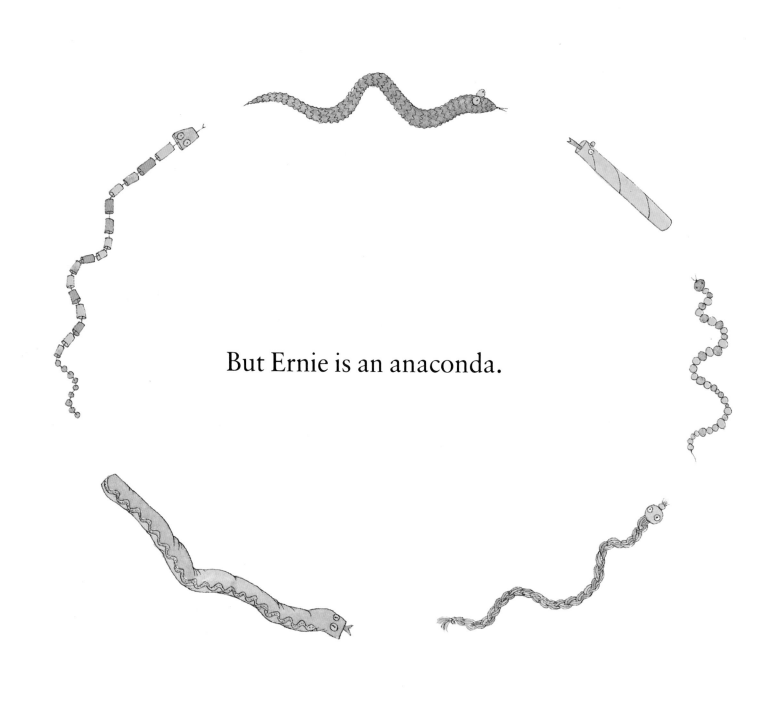

But Ernie is an anaconda.

Midnight Snacks

Celeste likes coconut macaroons.

Frank has stuffed olives.

Ernie eats the cooking chocolate.

Clive has a tube of
condensed milk.

Rosie likes
strawberry ice
cream.

Nicky has celery
with peanut butter.

But Tessa snaps snakes!